Acting Edition

Bite Me

by Eliana Pipes

D1606475

|| SAMUEL FRENCH ||

FOR PRODUCTION INQUIRIES

UNITED STATES AND CANADA
info@concordtheatricals.com
1-866-979-0447

UNITED KINGDOM AND EUROPE
licensing@concordtheatricals.co.uk
020-7054-7298

Each title is subject to availability from Concord Theatricals Corp., depending upon country of performance. Please be aware that *BITE ME* may not be licensed by Concord Theatricals Corp. in your territory. Professional and amateur producers should contact the nearest Concord Theatricals Corp. office or licensing partner to verify availability.

BITE ME was first produced by WP Theater (Producing Artistic Director, Lisa McNulty; Managing Director, Michael Sag) and Colt Coeur (Founding Artistic Director, Adrienne Campbell-Holt; Executive Producer, Heather Cohn) on September 22nd, 2023. The production was directed by Rebecca Martínez with scenic design by Chika Shimizu, costume design by Sarita Fellows, lighting design by Lucrecia Briceno, sound design by Tosin Olufolabi, and hair design by Ashley Wise. Fight and intimacy direction was by Judi Lewis-Ockler. The Production Stage Manager was Caren Celine Morris. The Assistant Stage Manager was Siobhan Petersen. The Prop Supervisor was Addison Heeren. The cast was as follows:

MELODY . . . . Malika Samuel
NATHAN . . . . David Garelik

BITE ME was originally workshopped and developed in the 2022 Pacific Playwrights Festival as part of The Lab at South Coast Repertory.

CHARACTERS

MELODY – Sixteen, Black, woman – Smart and outspoken (but never at the cost of being polite), a "good kid." Straight A's, a member of every student organization. She has a very organized backpack. Deeply isolated.

This high school is not in her district. She lives in a city closer to downtown than to the suburbs and makes a long commute by bus each morning and night. She sells homework to other kids under-the-table. Lately she's been crying through lunch.

MELODY – At twenty-seven in Act Two – Cold, self-protective, sharp-witted. Melody has become a confident and successful career woman, although navigating an elite university and the corporate world has hardened her spirit. She comes into the closet to flaunt her success, and to prove to herself that she's grown beyond the person she used to be in high school.

NATHAN – Sixteen, white, man – Charmingly arrogant and daring, a "bad kid." He can be perceptive, thoughtful, and kind, but he makes a point of doing it sparingly and only for people who've "earned" it. He has burgeoning alcoholism born from opportunity and angst. He comes from money but steals for sport.

NATHAN – At twenty-seven in Act Two – Warm, soft-spoken, unassuming. In the years after high school, Nathan hit rock bottom and undertook a humbling journey through substance abuse to recovery in a 12-Step Program. He thinks of Melody fondly and comes into the closet to make amends and to reconnect.

SETTING

A storage closet with a blue door at a suburban public high school in a "good" district.

This is a catch-all space at the school: theater costumes mingle with off-season sports gear and broken desks. Large wire racks hold boxes of junk. There's a dented metal table, and a rolling cart stacked with fold-up chairs.

TIME

Act One takes place in 2004.
Act Two takes place in 2015.

AUTHOR'S NOTES

Whenever possible, the play should be performed without an intermission.

A large asterisk in dialogue (*) indicates that the character is coughing or sneezing.

A forward slash (/) in dialogue indicates that the text immediately following is interrupted by another character's text in overlapping dialogue

For our younger selves
who carried us forward
and walk with us still

ACT ONE

Scene One

(The sound of a key turning in a lock –)

*(**MELODY** enters quickly and covertly. This is not her first time in the space, but she takes it in.)*

(She unstacks one of the folding chairs and sets it up at the metal table. She unzips her very organized backpack and takes out her lunch, something modest but healthy. She gets three bites in and stops herself cold. Then –)

(She starts crying, hard. It's weird and sad and endearing.)

(She attempts one more bite, then puts the food down altogether and indulges in the weeping. It almost seems like she's putting on a performance of crying, for herself.)

*(Suddenly – the lock starts to jiggle. **MELODY** freezes.)*

(She jumps to her feet and scans the room. She picks up a baseball bat instinctively for safety as a comfort object. She looks for a hiding spot, but just then –)

(The door swings open and **NATHAN** *is in the doorway, holding something rectangular under his shirt.)*

NATHAN. Melody?

MELODY. Oh, hi Nathan! / Uh –

NATHAN. What are you doing here?

MELODY. Did you follow me?

NATHAN. Wh–, no –

MELODY. What's under your / jacket? –

NATHAN. *(Seeing her food.)* Is that your lunch?

MELODY. No!

(The sound of footsteps approaching. **NATHAN** *leans out to trace the sound, then panics. He's only halfway through the door.)*

NATHAN. Fuck – uh, can I come in? I'm trying to lose this guy –

MELODY. Yeah, yeah, whatever –

(She moves her bag out of the way to make space for him. In the process, she also slams the lid on her lunchbox closed and shoves it back into her backpack.)

(He scoots inside and closes the door behind him quietly. Then presses his ear to the door to listen and waits.)

(Nothing for a moment. Then, distantly, the creeeeeeeak of a door opening. A few footsteps as someone surveys.)

*(***MELODY** *edges closer to the door and cranes her neck to try to hear the sound. She moves closer to him.)*

(The door handle jiggles, someone on the other side trying to get in. They both catch their breath. Then, it stops.)

(The distant door closes, and the footsteps drift away.)

(Whispering.) Who was that?

(He turns. They're face-to-face, and both surprised to find their bodies suddenly so close.)

(They linger there for a second. Heat. Then –)

NATHAN. Were you crying?

MELODY. What? No! – Um, it's just like, dusty in here –

*(**MELODY** breaks and makes distance between them. She realizes she still has the baseball bat in her hands.)*

Oh, I guess I should put this back.

Unless you need it for – whoever's out there?

NATHAN. No, I think I'm good.

(A little amused.)

Were you gonna hit me with that?

MELODY. No! Or – yeah?

Sorry – I like, panicked a little. I've never seen anyone in here before.

What are you doing in here?

NATHAN. Nothing. What are you doing?

MELODY. Nothing.

(Neither one knows what to say. They look at each other.)

> (**MELODY**'s *gaze lands on the object that* **NATHAN** *is hiding under his shirt. He shuffles his jacket to cover it.*)

NATHAN. Uh –

MELODY. Oh! Do you – um.

Do you want to take your worksheets now?

NATHAN. Oh –

MELODY. I know this isn't our usual trade-off time or whatever.

But I have them. In my bag. If you want.

NATHAN. I mean, whatever's good –

MELODY. Cool, yeah, let's do now! Right? Yeah!

Since we're both here, nice and convenient.

> (**MELODY** *goes to her backpack.*)

This is actually kinda lucky, I was running ahead of schedule this week. Usually I do them Thursday nights but I finished my English report early, which was a nice surprise. Or – it's whatever.

> (*While her back is turned,* **NATHAN** *focuses his attention on the thing under his shirt. He darts to one of the wire racks and uses his free hand to try to take down a specific box.*)

NATHAN. Cool. Is it still ten?

> (*Meanwhile* **MELODY** *pulls a folder out of one of the many, many zipper compartments of her bag.*)

MELODY. Actually it's fifteen now, because of the new like, little paragraph short answer thing that Mr. Hutchinson started adding. They just take a lot longer to do, and it's harder to reuse answers, and like – get my handwriting to look different.

NATHAN. Wait – you do different handwriting for every single one?

MELODY. Well, yeah of course.

> (*She turns around and locks eyes with* **NATHAN** *as he's trying to maneuver the box. He's caught.*)

What is that?

NATHAN. Nothing.

MELODY. Seriously?

> (*Beat.* **NATHAN** *reshuffles, seeming annoyed.*)

NATHAN. Do you have a – like a *reason* that you're in here?

MELODY. Oh – I just got the keys! I'm – um. Well it's complicated –

I'm on student council as the secretary and Kelly White used to be treasurer but she got walking pneumonia on her ski trip over winter break and so now I'm secretary *and* treasurer, and you get the key to this door so that you can get the lockbox down from storage for bake sales.

NATHAN. ...Okay.

So you're like *new*.

MELODY. New? To the room? Um. I guess.

NATHAN. It's just – I've kinda had this room for a while.

> (**MELODY** *stands her ground.*)

MELODY. Are you trying to like? – kick me out / right now?

NATHAN. No! But, I'm just saying, I do kinda have like a *stake* in this room.

We go way back, this room and me – like it's kinda *my* room.

MELODY. That's so funny, because *I* have the keys.

NATHAN. *(Accepting.)* Fair enough.

>   *(Beat.)*

MELODY. You can just tell me what you're doing, you know?

Like, it's cool.

I'm not gonna like tell the teacher on you, if that's what you're worried about –

NATHAN. I didn't think you would –

>   (**MELODY** *holds up the folder of plagiarized worksheets.)*

MELODY. I mean that should be obvious, I'm not a freaking narc, okay?

NATHAN. Okay, okay! –

MELODY. Like – you're good, that's all I mean.

NATHAN. Alright.

MELODY. So. Just tell me.

What is that? Did you take it?

>   (**NATHAN** *breaks into a devilish smile.)*

NATHAN. It's uh – it's kind of funny actually.

>   (**NATHAN** *lifts up his shirt to take the object out – and for a second,* **MELODY** *sees a flash of his bare chest.)*
>
>   *(He produces a huge framed glamour photo of a corgi, and a small generic award plaque.* **MELODY** *recognizes both objects immediately and rushes to them.)*

MELODY. No freaking WAY!!! Is this from the counselor's office?!? –

NATHAN. Yeah, this is Caputo's stupid little dog. Doesn't it look just like her? –

MELODY. Oh my god – a prize for "administrative excellence"? –

NATHAN. Yeah, she did an excellent job lecturing me –

MELODY. Wait, how did you even get this off the *wall*? –

NATHAN. Honestly? It's easier than you'd think. Nobody pays any fucking attention.

MELODY. Except for the guy that chased you here?

NATHAN. Yeah, except for him.

>   (*Beat.* **MELODY** *thinks.*)

MELODY. But – why'd you bring it all here?

NATHAN. Well. I uh – I have a little *collection*.

MELODY. Can I see it?

NATHAN. You want to?

MELODY. I mean, yeah.

>   (*Beat. He sizes her up.*)

NATHAN. Why were you crying?

MELODY. (*Firmly.*) I told you, I wasn't.

>   (**NATHAN** *points to her streaking makeup.*)

NATHAN. You have little like – lines, going on –

MELODY. Dammit!

>   (**MELODY** *turns and rubs under her eyes. She goes to her backpack and searches through the compartments until she finds a small compact. She checks herself in it.*)

NATHAN. So? I answered *your* question, didn't I?

MELODY. You did.

> (**MELODY** *sighs, she's not entirely out of the woods of this crying session.*)

It's stupid, I'm being stupid.

I just um. I heard some people talking shit about me and it got under my skin. That's all.

NATHAN. Who?

MELODY. That's two questions.

NATHAN. Just tell me.

MELODY. ....Jenny Wingate. And her stupid little posse – Tara and Celeste.

They do it, every week. Like, they'll talk shit about me while I'm in earshot.

And I know they do it just to get to me but it still does, like. Get to me.

> (**MELODY** *tears up again. She tilts her head back to stop her makeup from running and fans her eyes.*)

Sorry – this is so fucking embarrassing –

NATHAN. You need a cigarette.

MELODY. *(Laughing.)* I probably do.

> (**NATHAN** *swings his backpack off his shoulder and takes out a pack of cigarettes.* **MELODY** *stops cold.*)

Oh.

NATHAN. What?

MELODY. I just didn't think you like – had any.

NATHAN. Always.

> *(He opens the pack and takes out two cigarettes.)*

MELODY. How do you get them?

NATHAN. My brother picks them up for me, his ID says twenty-four.

Here, take it – it'll cool you down.

> *(He tucks one between his lips and holds another one out to her. She looks at it like it's a snake.)*

> *(Her eyes dart up to the ceiling.)*

MELODY. Um –

NATHAN. There aren't any smoke detectors if that's what you're looking for. I smoke in here all the time, I'm surprised you didn't smell it.

MELODY. I have kind of a bad nose.

NATHAN. You ever smoked before?

MELODY. *(Lying.)* Yeah!

NATHAN. Well, I'm not gonna tell on you either, if that's what you're worried about.

MELODY. I'm not worried.

NATHAN. No pressure or whatever, but like. It'll help.

> *(**MELODY** considers, then reaches for the cigarette. Then she stops herself.)*

MELODY. I don't think I could do a whole one by myself.

> *(He flashes her a smile, then puts the cigarette he'd offered her back into the pack. He takes the cigarette out of his mouth and hands that one to her instead.)*

NATHAN. I'll finish it for you.

> (*She takes it from him, very conscious that it just came out of his mouth. She puts it to her lips. He hands her the lighter, and she tries unsuccessfully to spark it.*)

MELODY. (*To herself, frustrated.*) I think it's sticking –

NATHAN. I got it –

> (**NATHAN** *steps in close to her. Heat.*)

> (*He takes the lighter and sparks it, using his other hand to cup the flame – even though there's no trace of a breeze in the still, silent room.*)

Okay, hold it up –

> (*She does. He lights the cigarette.*)

Now inhale.

> (*She does. He looks at the flame, she looks at him.*)

Now out.

> (*She exhales smoothly, using every molecule of her focus to keep herself from coughing. She produces a small puff of smoke. He's a little impressed.*)

Not bad.

> (*Now that she's passed his test –* **NATHAN** *goes back to the shelf and takes down the cardboard box he was reaching towards earlier.* **MELODY** *is a little proud of herself.*)

Anyway, Jenny Wingate is a fucking poser – I hate that bucktooth bitch.

MELODY. HA! Yeah – she IS a bucktooth – …

> *(She can't bring herself to say "bitch.")*

Yeah! I hate her too!

> (**NATHAN** *sets the box down on the ground.)*

NATHAN. There it is. My collection.

> (**MELODY** *moves to look at the box, amazed.)*

MELODY. Wow – this is…this is like…

NATHAN. *(Pointing to the cigarette.)* It's still lit.

MELODY. Oh!

> *(She tries another puff and immediately starts coughing.)*

(Coughs.) ***

NATHAN. You okay?

> *(She nods, but the cough is picking up. It's kind of intense.)*

Yeah, that'll happen.

MELODY. I'm – ** I'm good **** I just need to – ***

> *(She passes him the cigarette and goes to her backpack. She fishes out her water bottle and drinks deeply.)*

> *(He starts smoking effortlessly, taking long draws. He's clearly a smoker.)*

NATHAN. I used to cough too.

It's no big deal, like. I get it.

MELODY. Thanks.

It did help a little – I think. Or.

MELODY. I'm feeling better.

NATHAN. Good.

> (*Beat.* **MELODY** *looks to the box, his loot.*)

MELODY. Why don't you take them home? All this stuff? –

NATHAN. – I don't need it –

MELODY. Or like – sell them or something?

NATHAN. – I have money –

MELODY. But still, I bet you could pawn that plaque! And those jackets are really nice –

> (**NATHAN** *flips out his wallet and flashes it to her. It's packed with bills. It stops her cold.*)

Oh. Okay, got it.

...Then like – why keep it here?

> (**NATHAN** *smiles – good question.*)

NATHAN. Sometimes I put them back.

MELODY. (*She thinks.*) Like – if they deserve it?

NATHAN. Exactly.

> (*Heat. Then* **MELODY** *deflects.*)

MELODY. Can I ask you one more thing?

How did you get in this room? I'm the only student with a key.

> (*He reaches into his pocket, and takes out a Swiss Army Knife, then flicks open the blade.*)

You bring a knife to school every day?

NATHAN. It's just a Swiss Army knife.

MELODY. It's a knife. Like, I don't know the nuances or whatever, but that's a knife.

NATHAN. So?

MELODY. This school is crazy – in my old district we had random locker searches where you could get in trouble for having like craft scissors, and you bring a knife to school.

NATHAN. Does it scare you?

MELODY. That? No. Not really.

> (**NATHAN** *starts playing with the blade, doing weak attempts at knife tricks.* **MELODY** *is unfazed and holds his gaze.*)

NATHAN. *(Teasing her.)* My little tin blade doesn't intimidate you? Even though I'm a thief?

MELODY. I know how to fight.

NATHAN. It's sharp!

MELODY. I *know* how to fight.

> (*He drops the game and closes the blade.*)

NATHAN. I don't. Mostly used the bottle opener, but I don't drink beers much anymore.

> (*A shrill school alarm bell rings.*)

MELODY. Five minute bell. Lunch is almost over.

NATHAN. I'm done anyway.

> (**NATHAN** *snuffs out his cigarette and flicks it towards the windowsill.* **MELODY** *watches its path.*)

> (*He tosses the picture frame and plaque into his cardboard box and puts it back on the wire rack.*)

> (**MELODY** *goes back to the folder with his worksheets and takes out three sheets of paper.*)

MELODY. Oh, here you go –

NATHAN. Yes! Fifteen times three, right?

(*Too lazy to do the math.*) Fuck – what even is that?

MELODY. Forty-five.

NATHAN. Yeah, forty-five.

> (**NATHAN** *takes out his wallet and counts out the bills.* **MELODY** *starts to laugh to herself.*)

What?

MELODY. I'm just thinking – it's stupid.

NATHAN. *What?*

> (*She levels his gaze.*)

MELODY. I should've charged you more.

I mean, you've got a frikkin' treasure chest and a packed wallet and I said fifteen dollars?!

My rate is too low! That's like – so classic. Like, such a classic "me" problem.

Like, undervaluing myself –

NATHAN. Do you want more? I'll give you more if you want.

MELODY. No no! Sorry – it's more of like a general. Like. General epiphany.

Seriously, it's fine.

> (*He takes the worksheets, then hands her the bills.*)
>
> (*But when* **MELODY** *reaches out to take them,* **NATHAN** *doesn't let go. They stay there, connected.*)

(Heat.)

NATHAN. What do you want?

I'll get you something.

MELODY. Like…steal something? For me?

NATHAN. Yeah, as long as it's easy. We can call it payback, or like. Interest.

What do you want?

MELODY. What can I pick? Like – what's my range? I don't know what's easy to take.

NATHAN. I'll surprise you. Just – give me your favorite color or something.

MELODY. Blue.*

NATHAN. Okay. Back here on Tuesday.

MELODY. Okay.

> (**NATHAN** *grabs his bag and moves to leave. As he's halfway out the door,* **MELODY** *realizes something –)*

Wait –

Take it from Jenny.

Whatever it is – take it from Jenny.

NATHAN. *(Warmly.)* Deal.

> (*Once* **NATHAN** *is gone,* **MELODY** *goes to the spot where Nathan's cigarette fell and picks it up.)*

> (*Blackout.*)

---

* When **MELODY** tells **NATHAN** her favorite color here, it should be the same color as the dress she wears in Act Two – adjust the line to fit the costume.

Interlude I

(**MELODY** *stands at her locker and looks around to make sure she's alone.*)

(*She takes out a snack-sized Ziploc bag that's stuffed inside a quart-sized Ziploc bag [for a double-seal.]*)

(*The bag holds the cigarette butt that* **NATHAN** *flicked away in the storage closet. She saved it.*)

(*She takes a thin cardigan from her backpack and wraps it around the bag to stifle any smells, then stuffs it in the back of her locker.*)

(*She is exhilarated.*)

(*Blackout.*)

Scene Two

(The Storage Room.)

*(**MELODY** is sitting cross-legged on the dented metal table and peeling a tangerine.)*

(Her outfit is noticeably more embellished than in Scene One – a little collarbone showing, a special piece of jewelry. She dressed for this occasion and it shows.)

*(**NATHAN** sits nearby, looking the same as he did before. Today is not that kind of occasion for him. He's holding a cigarette and smoking as he speaks.)*

*(He's in the middle of telling a long story, loving the sound of his own voice. **MELODY**'s patience wears thin.)*

NATHAN. – and by that point in the night, Ryan was FUCKED up, like REALLY fucked up – and honestly I was pretty fucked up too, and so if he seemed fucked up by MY standards then he was REALLY fucked up, like this dude was on another PLANET –

MELODY. Why are you talking so loud?

NATHAN. What?

MELODY. You're like – shouting. I'm like three feet away from you.

NATHAN. I'm talking normal!

So anyway – Ryan is trying to go out with a *bang*, if you know what I mean. He's been to court-ordered rehab before and apparently it's a fucking drag, so he's trying to have a last hurrah, right? And he like, stumbles away from the pool to make a call and we lose track of him because my brother's losing his shit because Ryan got him all freaked out about shock treatment while he was tripping, so we had to calm him down. So *then* –

MELODY. Do you want some of my lunch? Because I packed extra.

NATHAN. Wh– no!

MELODY. How about just a cheese stick? It has protein!

NATHAN. No! I'm not hungry! Can you just stop / interrupting?

MELODY. Sorry, it's just like – been a minute and I don't see what this has to do / with –

NATHAN. The story is what *makes* it okay? Just, be patient.

So – Ryan's outside on the phone, and inside my brother is all tripping balls and crying, and me and the guys are like wasted but trying to cheer him up or whatever –

And then all of a sudden, guess who's pulling up to Ryan's party?

MELODY. Wait – sorry, it was Ryan's party?

NATHAN. Yeah.

MELODY. I thought you said it was your brother's party.

NATHAN. Well. Yeah, it was. It was technically a joint-party, like it was for Ryan because he got busted, but my brother threw it. Team effort.

MELODY. *(Skeptical.)* Okay.

NATHAN. So anyway – guess who pulls up to the party?

MELODY. *(Disinterested.)* Who?

NATHAN. Jenny. Fucking. Wingate.

(**MELODY** *leans in.*)

MELODY. Oh!!! Oh wait, she did –?

NATHAN. Yeah, fucking told you! So it turns out, Jenny's stupid friend with the mole –

MELODY. Celeste –

NATHAN. Yeah! Her and Ryan had this whole like *thing* going. So the Wingate crew rolls up together, like they always do, and they like descend on our party like fucking LOCUSTS, like a fucking *biblical plague*, they like sweep through the village and decimate our crops and they jack ALL OUR SHIT! We had like a fifth of vodka, which of *course* they drained, and then we had lines laid out and they like –

MELODY. Sorry – do you, like –? Do you really do all that?

      (Beat.)

Like – do you really drink that much? And like, do coke and stuff? Like, is that really like? Sorry – maybe I'm just dumb. But, I don't get how anybody could do all that and live.

      *(**NATHAN** smirks, and reaches into his backpack and takes out a shoulder of whiskey.)*

WHAT?! Are you serious, how do even *have* –?

NATHAN. I've got my brother's ID, and my parents don't give a shit.

MELODY. They really don't? Wow. My parents would kill me, honestly kill me.

NATHAN. Nah, Rob and Marsha have given up on me.

But it's fine. I'll die in my twenties and then they'll be sorry and that'll be my revenge.

      *(**MELODY** is surprised. He opens the bottle and drinks.)*

MELODY. Wait, you don't really –? You don't *mean* that, right?

NATHAN. I mean, I wouldn't be surprised.

MELODY. Why? Like why do you think you're gonna die in your twenties?

(He lifts up his hands with the whiskey bottle in one, and the cigarette in the other.)

NATHAN. Pick a hand.

MELODY. Well, put them down then!

NATHAN. Oh no, you don't understand – these are part of a strategy, live fast and die young.

MELODY. You don't actually think that, do you?

NATHAN. No, but don't I look like James Dean?

*(He poses. **MELODY** doesn't laugh.)*

MELODY. Who's that?

NATHAN. James Dean?

MELODY. Yeah, who is that?

NATHAN. You wouldn't get it.

*(**NATHAN** takes another drink. He's being a little dramatic, and he knows it.)*

MELODY. I'm serious – why don't you stop?

NATHAN. *(Somber, shrugging.)* Force of habit. I started too early.

MELODY. Well do you wanna like – quit?

NATHAN. Not particularly.

*(Beat. **MELODY** gets an idea. She puts her hand out.)*

MELODY. Well if you won't stop, then at least share it with me.

NATHAN. *(Puzzled.)* You don't have to like, take the hit for me you know. I'm fine.

This is kind of a light day for me, actually.

MELODY. I'm serious – hand it over.

NATHAN. Melody –

MELODY. Come on! All I have after lunch is free period, I just have to like – sit there.

Gimmie!

> (**NATHAN** *laughs, takes a swig, and then gives the bottle to her. She takes it, triumphantly.*)

Thank you.

> (**MELODY** *takes a small sip, then winces. She tries to cover it and takes another. She puts the bottle down.*)

You better not die any time soon, okay? I'm serious.

Like – I know I don't know you that well but like – just *don't* okay?

NATHAN. Okay, okay.

MELODY. I mean it – if you die I'll be like so annoyed with you!

(Softer.) I'll miss the fifteen bucks.

NATHAN. I won't. I promise.

MELODY. Good.

So, where were we?

NATHAN. Ryan's party – I'll cut to the chase. Basically, they all had too many vodka crans too fast, so while Jenny was ralphing in the bathroom, I grabbed this –

> *(He reaches into his backpack and tosses out a small makeup pouch.)*

NATHAN. For you.

> *(**MELODY** gasps and rushes to it.)*

MELODY. Oh-my-god-oh-my-god-oh-my-GOD!

NATHAN. That was worth the story, right?

MELODY. Yes! Like of *course*, this is TOO good – okay let's see –

> *(**MELODY** unzips the pouch and lays out the contents.)*

Chapstick, scrunchie – ooh, this is silk I think! Ew!! It still has her stupid hair in it!! A bracelet – is that turquoise?

NATHAN. I don't fuckin' know!

> *(**MELODY** takes a tin case out of the pouch.)*

MELODY. What's this?

> *(**NATHAN** takes the tin and pops it open.)*

NATHAN. They said they didn't bring anything – she was holding out on us!

MELODY. What is it?

> *(**NATHAN** holds the tin out towards her and she smells it.)*

Oh. They brought weed?

NATHAN. And didn't even offer it after they took ALL our shit!

MELODY. That's very inconsiderate.

NATHAN. Wanna try it?

(**MELODY** *is caught, referencing the bottle in her hands.*)

MELODY. Oh, I dunno.

NATHAN. No, it's perfect! You already learned how to smoke!

And this'll be more your style.

MELODY. *(Defensive.)* Why?

NATHAN. What do you mean?

MELODY. Like why more my style?

NATHAN. Because whiskey and cigarettes are for angry old men like me.

I'll stash it, it'll be here waiting for us.

(**NATHAN** *reaches up into the storage shelf and puts the tin into his cardboard box.*)

MELODY. You can keep it if you want! I don't mind.

NATHAN. No, I'll save it for next time!

MELODY. *(Smiling to herself.)* Okay. That sounds fun.

NATHAN. What else is in there?

(**MELODY** *reaches into the bag and pulls out the next item – but when she sees what's in her hands she flinches and drops it.*)

MELODY. AH!

(**NATHAN** *picks it up and howls with laughter.*)

NATHAN. A condom?

MELODY. Oh my god – why does she have that?

Do you think she's like… –

NATHAN. I doubt it – I think this is more aspirational.

(**MELODY** *remembers something.*)

MELODY. OH! Oh wait – oh my god you know what???

NATHAN. What?

MELODY. You know how she sits in front of me in Chem?

Well yesterday when you were absent, her and Tara only did like half of the in-class project that we had to do – like they didn't even *try*. But right before they handed it in, I watched them both put on this red lipstick and then, they kissed the cover page of their project before they turned it in.

(*She goes back into the pouch and finds a tube of drugstore lipstick.*)

NATHAN. (*Sound of disgust.*) Eugh.

MELODY. Yeah. And like, it wasn't a cute little kiss – it was like, mouth open, you know?

And when the projects got handed back, they got an A!

Mr. Hutchinson like – *gave them an A!!!*

Isn't that just –?? Like –??

(**MELODY** *stutters with feeling but falls silent.*)

NATHAN. Like what?

MELODY. It's just like – so fucking trashy. And unfair!

NATHAN. So, what? You think she's fucking Hutch?

I don't think he wears Magnums.

MELODY. EW! No! That's not what I mean! Just – they only did half the project and they got an A, like that's so fucking unfair.

(**NATHAN** *looks at her, amused by how passionate she is.*)

NATHAN. Hutch is a dirty old man and they're like, passably attractive. He probably whacks off to their ID photos at night when his stupid wife is knocked out on Ambien –

MELODY. UGH! Stop talking like that!!

NATHAN. Why does it freak you out so much? Are you a prude?

MELODY. No! Just they're like – children, and he's an old man! He's like a toad, it's disgusting, like why would they *invite* that? It's messed up.

NATHAN. I just think you're just jealous because they're smarter than you.

(*Beat.* **NATHAN** *is being smarmy, but this strikes a chord for* **MELODY**. *She's hurt.*)

MELODY. You think they're smarter than me?? Are you fucking kidding??

NATHAN. I mean, you're acing the class and they're acing the class – and they're not doing any work, so. Seems like their way is a little more – uh. Conservation of energy.

MELODY. First of all – that's Physics not Chemistry, dumbass –

NATHAN. (*Amused.*) Oh, good to know –

MELODY. And you know what? Why don't you pay them to do your Chem homework for you if you think they're so much smarter than me –

(**MELODY** *gets off the table and quickly gathers her things.*)

MELODY. Why don't you go to them for a lunchtime social hour / too, while you're at it –

NATHAN. Woah woah woah –

MELODY. Because honestly, you don't know shit about me –

> (**MELODY** *is poised to leave and* **NATHAN** *stands in front of the door to block her path.*)

NATHAN. WOW – fucking cool it okay! It was a JOKE!

Obviously they're not smarter than you, they have like seven brain cells between them and you're like already on track to cure cancer or something insane like that.

MELODY. No I'm not.

NATHAN. I'm just saying like. You know chemistry. That's not a bad thing. Jesus.

MELODY. *(Still upset.)* Sorry. That class is just – really hard.

> (**MELODY** *goes back to the bottle and takes another drink – a real one this time, a deep gulp. Then a smaller wince.*)

> (**MELODY** *sits on the table and tries to calm down.* **NATHAN** *gives her space.*)

I – uh. My parents had to petition to get me in at this school. It's not my district, I live down near Watkins so it's like, an hour each way on a bus. And all I do is study for that stupid class and I still don't really get it. And like, doing well here is really really important. So – um.

> (**MELODY** *takes a deep breath. This is hard for her to admit.*)

I cheat too.

NATHAN. You what?

MELODY. I cheat too. In Chem.

NATHAN. No way.

MELODY. *(She nods.)* I write the formulas on my leg with a marker. Like, high up.

And then I wear a skirt on the test days. So that I can peek, if I need help.

> *(Beat.)*

NATHAN. *That's* how you cheat? With like – references?

MELODY. It's still cheating!

NATHAN. Yeah but like – come on! Get some self-respect and cheat like an actual idiot –

> (**MELODY** *starts to laugh.*)

I mean it, you're just proving my point! Like, if you gave Jenny and Moleface the formulas they'd get nowhere! You're still *doing* chemistry.

MELODY. Well, they cheat like pretty girls.

NATHAN. Yeah, but – to be fair, your method does involve a short skirt.

> (**NATHAN** *sits on the table next to* **MELODY**. *Heat. Their bodies are so close. She screws up her courage:)*

MELODY. How come you never talk to me about Emmy?

> *(Beat.* **NATHAN** *freezes.)*

You talk about yourself all the time, but never her.

> *(Long beat.)*

You're still seeing her, right? Like, last I heard you guys were still together.

(**NATHAN** *gets off the table and starts to wander around the room. His demeanor changes.*)

NATHAN. No yeah, we're still going.

MELODY. And she's in college now?

NATHAN. Yup, second semester.

MELODY. Same year as your brother?

NATHAN. Yeah.

MELODY. College must be busy.

NATHAN. Jesus! How the hell do you know all this shit?

MELODY. It's just like, common knowledge. I dunno.

NATHAN. And hey – I do not talk about myself *all the time.* I make *conversation* because you're quiet.

MELODY. I'm not quiet! You just never ask me anything.

NATHAN. You need me to ask you stuff? You won't just bring things up like a normal person?

MELODY. You ask somebody how they're doing if you *really* want to know. It's polite.

　　　　(*Beat. He shifts.*)

NATHAN. Fine.

Are you fucking anybody?

MELODY. Oh my GOD – / NO!

NATHAN. Okay, okay! …

　　　　(*Loaded question.*)

Then do you have a crush?

MELODY. …Maybe.

NATHAN. Who is it?

MELODY. It's not important.

NATHAN. Who is it?

MELODY. You don't know him.

> *(He looks at her like she glints different in the light. She notices it.)*

> *(The bell rings.)*

NATHAN. Fuck, I'm gonna be late –

> (**NATHAN** *slings his backpack over his shoulder and grabs the bottle. He pulls out his BlackBerry and checks something.)*

MELODY. It's just the five-minute bell!

NATHAN. I know, but I have some business to sort out –

MELODY. Uh, okay – take these!

> (**MELODY** *pulls three worksheets from her backpack and hands them to* **NATHAN**.*)*

NATHAN. Thanks! I'll owe you for next time!

MELODY. Yeah, next time –

NATHAN. – and you're telling me about this guy okay? But I'll warn you, if he seems lame I'm gonna say it. Like I'm gonna be straight with you, I won't pad the truth.

MELODY. Okay, cool.

> (**NATHAN** *is halfway out the door, but he lingers in the doorframe.)*

NATHAN. And for the record?

If you felt like it – you could kiss your projects and get away with anything you wanted, you're hotter than bucktooth Jenny and Moleface. Even though you're basically a walking calculator.

(He leaves.)

(She stands up a little taller in the empty room.)

(Blackout.)

Interlude II

(*In Chemistry class, the middle of a test.* **NATHAN** *and* **MELODY** *sit in adjacent seats,* **MELODY** *wears a skirt.*)

(**MELODY** *is working intently, but* **NATHAN** *seems lost and distracted. His eyes flit to her test.*)

(*He checks to make sure the teacher isn't watching, then taps his pencil eraser on his desk to get* **MELODY***'s attention. She notices him. They stay aware of the teacher at the front and whisper:*)

NATHAN. Number four?

(**MELODY** *checks her test and whispers back:*)

MELODY. B –!

NATHAN. D –?

MELODY. B –!!

(*Suddenly,* **MELODY** *sits up a little straighter in her chair. She reaches down and uses one hand to gather up the material of her skirt, exposing her upper thigh.*)

(**NATHAN** *is surprised and intrigued.*)

(*She uses her fingernail to slowly draw the letter on her leg – "B." He watches her.*)

NATHAN. Thanks.

(*She plays it off with a shrug and turns back to her test. After a second, she breaks out in a smile. He smiles too.*)

(*Blackout.*)

Scene Three

(The Storage Room.)

*(The joint is lit and in circulation. **NATHAN** is looking gaunt and exhausted. He tries to keep his spirits up.)*

*(**MELODY** is holding her water bottle, prepared for coughing this time. She's feeling up and confident. It suits her.)*

(She has a photo pulled up on her flip phone and holds it tight to her chest.)

MELODY. OKAY! Before you look, I just want to say that he's like *really* sweet –

NATHAN. If you're giving a disclaimer then he's definitely ugly.

MELODY. No he is not! I just don't think you're gonna be fair! / You're like a biased jury –

NATHAN. I'm very fair – wait, biased how?

MELODY. *(Giggling.)* I dunno!

(She references the joint.) Wow, I do like this! You were right!

NATHAN. You know, most people don't really get high their first time.

MELODY. Whatever – give it back.

*(**MELODY** reaches for the joint and he takes one last draw. She gets a good look at him and seems concerned.)*

Are you okay?

NATHAN. Yeah, why?

MELODY. You look kind of like. Pale and glassy.

NATHAN. I always look like this.

MELODY. You're like skin and bones.

NATHAN. I'm chiseled, I have cheekbones.

MELODY. I have a chicken sandwich, you can have half if you want!

(*He rolls his eyes and passes her the joint.*)

NATHAN. You're stalling. This guy must be a fuckin' dog.

MELODY. He is not!! I just don't know why you get to be the judge all of a sudden –

NATHAN. Because you don't know shit about relationships.

MELODY. Um ouch.

NATHAN. I am sort of the expert here! Admit it! Me and Emmy have been together THREE years, okay! She changed schools, I moved further away – STILL stayed together. And that's just like statistical quantifiable information, like irrefutable. I have expertise on this subject. Thank you.

MELODY. Okay FINE.

(*She takes a last puff. She's not actually all that high, but she's enjoying the thrill and the psychosomatic effects.*)

(*Then she turns her flip phone around, revealing a pixelated image of a boy. She hands the phone to* **NATHAN.**)

Do you know Edwin Alfortson?

NATHAN. *Edwin.*

MELODY. Yeah.

NATHAN. His name is *Edwin*?

MELODY. He can't help his name!

NATHAN. Yeah but if your name is *Edwin* and you don't go by Eddie then you're probably a fucking psychopath.

MELODY. Okay – fine! But do you know him –?

NATHAN. Sorta – we're both in Croland's English. How'd you get this picture?

MELODY. Don't worry about it.

NATHAN. *(He considers.)* Okay. Not as bad as I thought, honestly. He kinda dresses like a d-bag, I'm not gonna lie to you here –

MELODY. I know, I see it –

NATHAN. But he also seems kind of creative, which is cool. Like he has those hats –

MELODY. Yeah!

NATHAN. Like he's *trying* but it's got a flair to it that I can sort of respect.

MELODY. He is! Creative, I mean. He draws and stuff. He's doing like a skateboard design thing.

NATHAN. *(Quietly.)* Oh, he's a skater? You better get some knee pads.

MELODY. What?

NATHAN. Never mind. Is his hair always like that?

MELODY. I like his hair.

> (**NATHAN** *scrutinizes the image, looking for a flaw.*)

NATHAN. Isn't he friends with that weird kid? What's his name –?

MELODY. They're not friends anymore.

NATHAN. Oh and what the hell is this?! Fur lining on his hoodie? Be cold like a man!

MELODY. Well I don't mind it! I like him.

> (**MELODY** *takes her phone back from him.*)

And I think he maybe likes me.

We've been talking on AIM and I think we're gonna like – *see* each other next week.

> (*A shift in* **NATHAN.**)

NATHAN. Is he taking you somewhere?

MELODY. To Main Street. I've never been.

NATHAN. You've never been to Main Street?

MELODY. I live in Watkins, remember?

NATHAN. Right, right.

(Annoyed.) Well. Good. Great. Just. If he fucking sucks, just know I told you so.

Like – obviously I hope it goes well and good luck or whatever, but if he's a piece of shit then I'm gonna say I told you so and you can't blame me.

MELODY. Sure, yeah. Whatever.

> (*Beat.*)

Oh! I waved to you in the hall today, I don't know if you saw me.

NATHAN. I guess not.

MELODY. Why do you wear sunglasses during passing period?

NATHAN. So I don't have to make eye contact.

> (*Beat.*)

MELODY. Are you sure you're okay? You look terrible.

NATHAN. So do you.

MELODY. Very funny. I actually kind of tried today. Got these new Keds!

>   *(She swings her foot out to show him the shoes.)*

They're not like Air Force Ones or whatever, but I like them. They're canvas so it's hard to keep them clean. I think I'm gonna bleach them.

>   *(Beat.)*

Sorry – just. Are you sure you're good? You're really quiet.

NATHAN. I'm fine. Just didn't sleep much, that's all. Took my Addy too late.

MELODY. Oh. Do you need to sleep, or –?

NATHAN. No, I had a coffee, I'll crash when I'm home.

The other day Emmy was telling me that she thinks her natural state is nocturnal, and honestly I think I'm the same way. I'd so much rather sleep all day and stay up all night.

Not have to deal with people all the time.

>   *(**MELODY** breaks into a huge grin.)*

What?

>   *(She tries to stop herself from laughing.)*

Oh my god, what is it?

MELODY. Um. Emmy didn't tell you that story. I did.

NATHAN. You did?

MELODY. Mhm. Last time, remember? I was talking about how I stay up until I hear everyone else in the apartment go to bed, I wait until I can't hear the footsteps anymore. It was me.

NATHAN. Oh. I guess I forgot.

MELODY. Yeah, guess so.

So you're welcome I guess for that fun little story. Glad you agree.

NATHAN. Okay, settle down champ.

MELODY. Whatever, I'm not the one mixing names up!

> (**MELODY** *takes another small puff of the joint.*)

Whewh – I think I'm gonna stop.

> (**NATHAN** *takes the joint back.*)

NATHAN. You're fine.

MELODY. Yeah, no – I feel good.

> *(Beat.)*

Does she know? Like. About this? Like that we – have lunch?

NATHAN. Yeah.

MELODY. *(Surprised.)* Oh. And it doesn't like, bother her?

NATHAN. No, not really.

MELODY. *(Disappointed.)* Oh.

NATHAN. Because like, we're friends. I told her that.

MELODY. Yeah, no, whatever – I get it. I'm not a threat. I get it.

NATHAN. Oh my god, don't do that. And can we like, stop talking / about her?

MELODY.   I mean, that's not like an interpretive breakthrough, like, that's what she means.

That's what she means by that.

NATHAN.   No it's not – Emmy's just – we've been through shit you know? Like her bar for suspicion is just – in a different place. She doesn't get nervous unless I'm blacked out in a ditch.

MELODY.   Wait, do you do that?

NATHAN.   Don't worry about it. But the point is like. *That's* not why Emmy isn't nervous.

And can we just. Drop it.

MELODY.   Fine.

NATHAN.   You have like – *Edwin.*

MELODY.   *(Undecided.)* Yeah. I dunno.

NATHAN.   What?

MELODY.   I dunno.

NATHAN.   Oh my god it is so annoying when you do that.

MELODY.   I dunno about like. If I even want to be dating anybody at all.

NATHAN.   Why not?

MELODY.   I dunno. It's stupid.

NATHAN.   Come on! You say I don't ask you stuff, I'm asking. What is it?

> *(She takes a deep breath and tries to find her words.)*

MELODY.   Okay – like. Okay.

So my upstairs neighbors, this young couple – I've seen them a few times and they look, like *so* in love, all hanging on each other, lovey-dovey. But the walls are really thin, and sometimes I can hear them and the sounds are like – there's like hitting and yelling and growling and like things crashing –

NATHAN. ...So are they fucking?

MELODY. Well that's the thing! I can't tell. I can't tell if it's like – sex, or like...violence.

NATHAN. Oh.

MELODY. Like sometimes she screams like she just got punched in the face, and it's like *oh my god* – do I need to call somebody? Or, there'll be a crash and it's like, did a chair fall over? Or was that like, *her* body getting knocked onto the ground?

It sounds so fucking terrible.

But sometimes it's a like – a happy scream, like a *thrill*. And I'm like, wait. Like, is she crying, or is that – giggling? Did he knock her over, or did she like, knock him onto the bed? The line is so thin. I keep trying to figure out what's going on up there –

NATHAN. *(With innuendo.)* ...You're trying to picture it?

MELODY. Wh–, I mean – no! Just like. Trying to make sense of the sounds, like. Synthesize the information.

NATHAN. *(Still joking.)* Oh, you wanna *synthesize* it?

MELODY. I'm serious! That's not what I mean! Like – it's the opposite actually. They make me want to like – go be a monk and live in a hollowed-out mountain or something. Like, my self-preservation instinct kicks in and just goes on overdrive and says no.

> (**MELODY** *fans herself a little. She notices that she's sweating a little bit.*)

Oh wow, this is crazy, I'm talking so much –

I don't think I've ever talked this much before, like all at once?

NATHAN. What – you think little Edwin with the fur-lined coat is gonna like, hit you or something?

MELODY. No, no! But like. That happens! You know? That happens.

Have you ever looked at the statistics on like – violence? My mom is really into statistics.

Like, okay – if I wasn't here I'd be at Burroughs High in the city and like six of those girls got pregnant last year. Six. This girl from my old dance class, she has a baby now – it was like: boyfriend, then BOOM. We had all these big dreams you know? I promised myself I'd keep in touch with those girls but now there's just nothing left to say.

> (**NATHAN** *takes a big puff of the joint, and then lets the smoke hang in the air for a moment.*)

NATHAN. Who cares about those girls at Burroughs?

> (**MELODY** *is thrown.*)

MELODY. Who *cares*?

NATHAN. Yeah. That has nothing to do with you.

You're not like them.

MELODY. Yes I am, I'm exactly like them.

NATHAN. You don't go there anymore, you go here.

MELODY. But that's the only difference.

NATHAN. Burroughs has nothing to do with you, that statistic has nothing to do with you.

MELODY. Yeah – but what if I went back?

What if I get caught cheating or selling worksheets and I get expelled and then I'm back in my home district. The formula is: I come out here to the better school,

I get good grades, so that I can make it into a good college, and have a good future. But what if I go back? Like, solve for x.

NATHAN. You're a fucking microchip!

MELODY. And anyway it's like – not. It's not about that it's about like – …

NATHAN. What?

MELODY. I dunno. I lost the thought.

> *(Beat.)*

Those neighbors upstairs? Those two kinds of screams?

My parents are like, the opposite.

I mean I know they love each other, but it's not like *love* love, you know? There's no spark.

Even when my parents get mad there's no spark!

They just go quiet, like no one talks at all.

NATHAN. They don't yell at you?

MELODY. No, never.

NATHAN. Well, some people just – yell. My parents yell all the time. It's not a big deal, it's just how they talk. That's life I guess. Or like – that's love.

MELODY. If *that's* love then like – why should I?

Screaming, or silence, or getting pregnant?

Like, if those are my options, I don't want any of it.

NATHAN. I don't think it's that simple.

MELODY. I guess.

Is it like that for you and Emmy?

NATHAN. *(He sighs.)* Me and Emmy, we're like – I wasn't gonna say anything but –

NATHAN. We're like. We're on a break *thing* right now.

> (*He hits the joint with pointed frustration.*
> **MELODY** *perks up, but tries to cover.*)

MELODY. A break?

NATHAN. She got involved with some fuckin' college guy with a messenger bag or something.

I know she just did it because she was bored. But like. Whatever.

MELODY. I'm so sorry. That's bullshit.

NATHAN. Yeah, it's fine. We don't have to like, talk about it. It's the least of my problems anyway.

MELODY. What happened?

> (**NATHAN** *takes a long hit. He opens up.*)

NATHAN. (*Sighs.*) My idiot brother got himself arrested.

MELODY. Oh I'm so sorry – that's awful.

NATHAN. After Ryan got caught he knew he had to be careful, but no – he just couldn't fucking do it. He just landed in rehab, gone for three months.

MELODY. Oh. Well at least it's not too long!

NATHAN. It's fucking forever when half your customers want to kill you! We've been selling my Adderall prescription and his Ritalin – and I can't even buy through Emmy's college dealer with this stupid fucking "break" thing, it's a nightmare. Like now I have to figure this shit out all alone –

MELODY. You're not alone.

> (*Their eyes meet for a moment. Heat.*)

NATHAN. Actually – do you still have that sandwich?

MELODY. Oh – yeah!

(**MELODY** *reaches into her lunch box and takes out half her sandwich – a significant portion of her lunch for the day.*)

(*She moves toward* **NATHAN** *to hand him the sandwich, then curls up next to him. He takes it and scarfs it down.*)

NATHAN. *(Sincerely.)* Thank you.

MELODY. Of course.

(*They sit in silence, chewing. It's comfortable and close.*)

You know what I keep dreaming about?

NATHAN. What?

MELODY. Wearing Jenny's bracelet. Like here, in the middle of the day, in front of her.

I wear it at home sometimes, like just to feel what it's like, you know?

But I'd love to wear it here.

NATHAN. You should.

MELODY. I mean, I can't. It's stolen.

NATHAN. Yeah, but she could never call you on that.

I stole it and I gave it to you – you're not guilty.

MELODY. Wouldn't it like – blow your cover?

NATHAN. She doesn't even know that we know each other.

MELODY. I guess that's true. Oh my god, she'll be like, "Omg where did you get that?" and I'll be like, "Oh? This little thing? I just picked it up at the mall, I don't even remember."

NATHAN. Do it! Wear it!

MELODY. You know what, yeah! I will!

>   (**MELODY** *reaches into her backpack and
>   takes out the stolen makeup pouch. She
>   removes the small gold chain bracelet and
>   puts it on her wrist.*)

NATHAN. You deserve it.

These fuckers don't deserve anything. You know what,
here –

>   (**NATHAN** *goes to the wire rack and takes his
>   large cardboard box off the shelf.*)

MELODY. What are you doing?

>   (*He opens the box and tosses it to the center of
>   the space.*)

NATHAN. Take it, take anything.

MELODY. Any of it?

NATHAN. Yeah, why not. Here – denim jacket, you want
this?

MELODY. Sure!

NATHAN. It's yours.

>   (**NATHAN** *takes the denim jacket out for*
>   **MELODY**. *She takes it, then joins him in
>   sorting through the box.*)

MELODY. Ooh – pencil case?

NATHAN. Take it –

MELODY. Who did it even belong to?

NATHAN. I don't remember anymore, it doesn't matter.
Here –

MELODY. What else you got?

*(Something in the far corner of the box catches **MELODY**'s eye, and she reaches to get it. **NATHAN** plays a game of keep-away with her, pulling the box just out of her reach.)*

*(When **MELODY** lunges for the box, her body crosses over **NATHAN**'s – and they both suddenly become very aware of their closeness.)*

(They look to each other, she's almost sitting in his lap.)

(Heat.)

*(Then **MELODY** deflects, turning her focus back to the box.)*

This notebook is nice, oh look someone sketched in it!

Seems like mostly English notes but maybe we can find something –

(Then, he puts his arms around her waist and pulls her a little closer. Their bodies touch.)

(She adjusts to face him, neither of them seem confident in their movements but they're trying to stay close – they look like they're in a strange game of Twister, but this is a new level of physical intimacy, especially for her.)

(The cardboard box blocks the audience's view of most of their bodies – all we see is this strange closeness.)

(Blackout.)

Interlude III

*(In the morning, **MELODY** stands at a bathroom mirror getting ready for the day – decking herself out in the stolen goods from the storage room.)*

(She wears Jenny's bracelet, Harrison's denim jacket, Celeste's tank top, a silver ring belonging to god knows who, and on and on and on.)

(The items are all somewhat mismatched, and don't quite fit her properly, but she doesn't mind. She feels good.)

*(**MELODY** gets an idea. She puts on Jenny's stolen lipstick and pulls out a piece of notebook paper. Then she plants a kiss on it leaving a lipstick kiss mark behind.)*

*(At school, **MELODY** makes a show of strutting down the hall for her imaginary classmates, standing tall.)*

*(**NATHAN** appears at the other side of the hall, wearing his sunglasses. **MELODY** waves to him. He doesn't seem to see. She waves again. Again, nothing.)*

*(**NATHAN** approaches **MELODY**, she smiles and gets ready to hand him the kiss note, but instead he walks past her without any acknowledgement.)*

*(**NATHAN** exits, **MELODY** deflates a bit. She looks back to the kiss note, and follows him.)*

(Blackout.)

Scene Four

(The Storage Room.)

*(**MELODY** enters, very on edge, almost shaking.)*

*(She's holding on to a pair of expensive aviator sunglasses, the same pair we've seen on **NATHAN**.)*

(She paces and fidgets, looking for something to do with all the excess energy.)

*(Then, **NATHAN** comes in behind her, also deeply on edge. They're both heated.)*

NATHAN. What the hell was / that?

MELODY. I'm sorry, I just needed to / talk to you –

NATHAN. You can't just like – *do* shit like that Melody / what the fuck –

MELODY. I said I was sorry –

NATHAN. Where are my glasses?

MELODY. Here, here –

> *(**MELODY** takes them out of her bag and gives them to him.)*

NATHAN. Those are fucking expensive you know –

MELODY. I was gonna give them back –

NATHAN. You can't just like, take them off my head in the hallway, like that was really fucking weird, everyone saw you –

MELODY. Well you've been avoiding me for weeks / what was I supposed to do?

NATHAN. I'm not avoiding you I'm just busy!

MELODY. Busy doing what?

NATHAN. Who cares what – are you a fucking cop? I'm busy!

MELODY. It's been like *three weeks* Nathan.

NATHAN. No it hasn't.

MELODY. It has!! Look –

> (**MELODY** *goes to her backpack and takes out a stack of worksheets, her evidence.*)

I was gonna give you these, all these worksheets!

> (*She counts them out.*)

Three – six – nine! See! Three weeks' worth!! It's been three weeks!

NATHAN. So what, you're here to shake me down for cash, is that it? Fine –

> (**NATHAN** *takes out his wallet.*)

MELODY. No, it's not about the money –

NATHAN. No – go ahead, what do I owe you –

> (**MELODY** *sees a bright red, angry burn mark on the top of* **NATHAN**'s *hand. It stops her in her tracks.*)

MELODY. Oh my god –

NATHAN. What?

> (*Beat.* **MELODY** *can't take her eyes off the burn on his hand.*)

MELODY. What is that?

NATHAN. What?

MELODY. On your hand.

> *(He tries to hide it.)*

NATHAN. Cigarette burn, it's nothing.

MELODY. It looks so red.

> *(Instinctively she moves toward* **NATHAN** *and holds his palm with both hands.)*
>
> *(***MELODY*** catches his hand before he can move away from her.* **NATHAN** *is caught in the tenderness of her touch.)*
>
> *(She studies the burn closely.)*

Who did this?

NATHAN. I did.

MELODY. You burned yourself?

NATHAN. It was a joke.

MELODY. It's not very funny.

NATHAN. I'm not very funny.

MELODY. What is going on with you?

Are you alright?

> *(He pulls his hand away from her and goes cold.)*

NATHAN. So what is it? What's the big fucking problem?

Is this about that guy?

MELODY. Edwin? No – that's like, *over.*

NATHAN. *(Suspicious.)* Over?

MELODY. It was just –

> *(Her face twists up.)*

MELODY. It's fine, don't worry about / it –

NATHAN. What did he do? Do you need me to kick his ass
   or / something because if that's what this is about then
   you can just get to it –

MELODY. Wh– no! That's not what I –!

   (Overpowering him.) He kissed me! That's all. We
   kissed.

NATHAN. Oh.

MELODY. My first kiss.

      (Beat.)

NATHAN. How was it?

MELODY. Bad. I mostly just tasted his lunch. He had a
   turkey sandwich with like, a LOT of yellow mustard.
   I think his tongue was yellow.

NATHAN. I told you so.

MELODY. I guess. It's like. I wanted it to be magic, but it
   was just...spit.

NATHAN. You gonna see him again?

MELODY. No, he stopped messaging me back last week.
   That's why it's over.

   I probably shouldn't be surprised.

      (Beat.)

NATHAN. *(Harshly.)* Just – tell me what you need, okay?
   You already got me down here so just fuckin' get to it.

MELODY. *(Flustered.)* Sorry – I, I guess I just –

      (She collects herself.)

   Can you read something for me?

NATHAN. Read something?

MELODY. I – um. Okay.

> (**MELODY** *turns and searches through her backpack.*)

Things have been, uh – getting worse with Jenny and Celeste lately.

Just like – meaner and more specific, and it's sticking in my head more. Today in Chem they were passing notes, and I can't tell you why, but I knew that it was about me. I could feel it. So I stayed back after class and I fished it out of the trash can like a psycho.

> (**MELODY** *takes out a small piece of pink paper, covered in gel pen writing.*)

NATHAN. Jesus.

MELODY. I know.

Got fucking ketchup on my nice sweater.

NATHAN. Melody, this is – like.

MELODY. I know, I know, it's like – bad. But I just, need to know.

Will you read it for me?

> (*She holds the note out to him, he steps back from it.*)

NATHAN. Wh– no!

MELODY. *Please* Nathan, just – read it.

Read it and tell me what it says. Or like –

Tell me if I can handle it. Tell me if it's true.

NATHAN. Who gives a shit what it says –!

MELODY. I do –!

NATHAN. It's probably not even about you –!

MELODY. Then prove me wrong, okay? Just, please. I don't want to do it alone.

MELODY. Will you read it?

> (**NATHAN** *sighs, then approaches the piece of pink paper. He unfolds it.* **MELODY** *watches him with laser-focus, holding her breath.*)
>
> (**NATHAN** *reads the note.*)
>
> (*Then, the life drains from his face. He reads on, more life drains. Suddenly – he tears the letter into shreds.*)
>
> (**MELODY** *lunges to stop him –*)

What the hell are you / doing??!

NATHAN. / You don't need this shit!

MELODY. Why did you do that??

NATHAN. Listen to me, ignore them, ignore it – okay? It's / not about you –

> (**MELODY** *drops to her knees and gathers the scraps of the note from off the floor.* **NATHAN** *tries to pull her away.*)

Fuck that and fuck them!

MELODY. No – no – no – / no – no –

NATHAN. Just let it go, I'm doing you a favor!

MELODY. That's not / the point –!

NATHAN. Just leave it, it doesn't matter – it's not about you!

MELODY. (*Overpowering his voice.*) I know that!

> (*Beat.*)

It's about *you*.

(**MELODY** *stops trying to reassemble the note and stays on the ground trying to steady herself.* **NATHAN** *is shocked.*)

NATHAN. What?

MELODY. Why did you tear it up? That's not what you were supposed to do!

NATHAN. Supposed to –? What do you mean?

MELODY. Dammit –

NATHAN. Melody, what the hell are you talking about?

(**MELODY** *sits up with her face streaked in tears. She recites the note, word-for-word, in monotone. She's shaking.*)

MELODY. "Did you see Smellody trying to eye-fuck Nathan in passing period? Hilarious."

"After Edwin had one taste and spit her back out, now she's gonna swing for Nathan?"

"And she's dressing like a hooker now. Probably for him, / as if."

NATHAN. / You read it?

MELODY. "And the perfume! No matter what she does she always smells like beef"

NATHAN. / Hey – stop that –

MELODY. "Or like – cat food. I wonder if that's what she eats out in the wild."

NATHAN. Stop doing that!! Fuck.

(**MELODY** *turns to look at* **NATHAN**.)

MELODY. You know what's funny? This is *her* shirt.

Celeste thinks I look like a hooker and this is *her* fucking shirt.

MELODY. You took it, and gave it to me. I've been wearing
  her shirt, and Jenny's bracelet, and

  Harrison's jacket, and these stupid silk scrunchies –

  And I was so ready to like – bask in it.

  But nobody even noticed.

  Nobody.

> *(Beat.)*

NATHAN. Why did you read it?

MELODY. Why did you burn your hand?

> *(Beat.)*

> *(**NATHAN** breaks their gaze. He sighs and
> paces around the space. **MELODY** keeps her
> eyes fixed on him.)*

> *(**NATHAN** tries to be comforting, but there's a
> whiff of exasperation in his voice.)*

NATHAN. Look, those girls are fucking idiots, okay?

  You just – you can't let shit like this get to you, alright –

  Forget about them, tune them out – it doesn't matter!

  You're smart and you're cool, and you're funny, who
  gives a fuck what they think!

> *(**MELODY** stands, trampling the torn-up note,
> and zeroes in on **NATHAN**.)*

MELODY. *You* do.

  You give a fuck what they think.

> *(Heat – but not the same kind.)*

NATHAN. *(Surprised.)* N– No I don't!

MELODY. Yes you do! You obviously do!

NATHAN. Bucktooth Jenny and Moleface? No way!

MELODY. You *do* care what they think of you –

NATHAN. Hey – I'm not hung up on what *anybody* thinks, alright –?

MELODY. You don't talk to me out there! You don't!

(*She points to the door.*)

Outside that blue door, you pretend like I don't exist. Why?

(*Beat – he falters.*)

NATHAN. Because – that's just – that's different –

I pretend like everybody doesn't exist, that's my deal.

MELODY. But that's not the same thing!

NATHAN. How is it not?

MELODY. Because I'm not like everyone else! I think you maybe *know* me, Nathan – like who I actually am. Nobody else here really knows me.

And the way we talk in here? Is like – real. So then – what is it?

(*She waits.*)

Why won't you even look at me out there?

(**MELODY** *looks to him for an answer.*)

(**NATHAN***'s face darkens and twists – in an instant it's like a storm cloud has arrived over his head.*)

(*He pulls back from her.*)

NATHAN. So what – this whole thing was some kind of little test?

>*(Beat.)*

MELODY. What?

NATHAN. You lied about reading that note!

Or you know what, maybe the better word is trap –

This is a / fucking ambush!

MELODY. It was not! You're just trying to change the subject!

NATHAN. What the hell was I "supposed to" say exactly?

After that little / performance?

MELODY. I just thought – that you'd – *help*, I dunno!

I felt like shit, I thought you'd make me feel better, I just – I needed a friend –

NATHAN. You want me to rip Jenny off again, is that it?

Steal you another lipstick?

MELODY. Why are you being an asshole / right now?

NATHAN. Look, I don't know what you thought this was,

But I'm not your little boyfriend or whatever, okay?

I don't like you like that!

>*(Beat.)*

>*(**MELODY** is struck by his coldness, but she stays firm. She's working hard to hold herself together.)*

MELODY. *(Level.)* That's not true.

NATHAN. What?

MELODY. Tell the truth –

NATHAN. Are you serious?

MELODY. It's not true. Just admit it, come on –

NATHAN. Look, I don't know what kind of delusional / fantasy –

MELODY. *(Blurting it out.)* I know because I felt your hard-on through your jeans when you grabbed me three weeks ago.

>	*(Thicker air.)*

NATHAN. How the hell would you even know what it feels like for someone to want you?

Huh? Little virgin Melody? Now you're some kind of expert?

>	*(He laughs at her.)*

What a fucking joke! I mean, when you flashed me in Chem I just thought it was funny, and then all of a sudden you threw your ass at me in here three weeks ago – but did you *actually* think –? That I would *ever*?

>	*(He goes to his wallet.)*

You know what – how about we square up right now.

MELODY. *(To herself.)* I don't care about the money –

>	*(**NATHAN** opens his wallet and throws a fistful of bills at her. **MELODY** flinches and protects her face.)*

>	*(She gasps.)*

>	*(The bills waft down to the floor around her, landing among the scraps of the torn-up note.)*

>	*(**NATHAN** is breathless, like a child after a tantrum.)*

NATHAN. Enjoy – We're even –

You're just the girl that does my Chem homework, okay? That's it.

> *(He breaks and moves to the steel table and kicks one of the chairs – it falls and clatters onto the floor.)*

> *(**NATHAN** sweeps up his backpack and heads for the door.)*

(Muttering to himself.) You know what, fuck this –

> *(**MELODY** stares him down as he goes – she stays frozen to the spot, but she makes an effort to stand tall.)*

> *(**NATHAN** stumbles with the doorknob at first and kicks the door frame hard – then he pulls again and then the door swings open.)*

> *(He leaves – and **MELODY** flinches as the door slams behind him.)*

> *(She stands alone in the room, on the torn-up remains of the passed note – looking suddenly small in the space.)*

> *(Blackout.)*

Interlude IV

(In the moments after **NATHAN** *slams the door.)*

*(***MELODY** *–)*

(Stands in the storage closet, trying to hold herself together. She slowly picks up the money that Nathan threw at her, collecting it from the ground.)

*(***NATHAN** *–)*

(Enters the parking lot, still buzzing with energy. He takes out a cigarette and searches for his lighter. He checks his coat and pants pockets, no –)

(Then he reaches into his backpack and sees something that surprises him. He takes out a folded up piece of lined notebook paper and hesitantly unfolds it.)

(It's the note with Melody's lipstick kiss. He takes it in.)

*(***MELODY** *–)*

(Is buzzing with energy too, she's overcome with feeling and tries to shake off the emotion. She suddenly drops to the floor and does sit-ups.)

MELODY. One – two – three –

(She stops, the sit-ups are not helping, she's too upset.)

(*NATHAN –*)

(*Softens in an instant, for a moment he's hit with a pang of regret.* **NATHAN** *looks around to make sure he's alone. And he is.*)

(*He studies the note closely. With the lightest touch in the world, he gently runs his finger over the lipstick mark.*)

(*MELODY –*)

(*Turns and looks back to the door.*)

(*She wonders if Nathan might return, might come to his senses and apologize. She waits for a moment, hoping.*)

MELODY. (*To herself.*) Nathan –

(*But nothing happens. She approaches the door.*)

(*NATHAN –*)

(*Suddenly stands, ashes out his cigarette, and leaves.*)

(*MELODY –*)

(*Presses her ear to the door, desperate to hear footsteps.*)

(*Then she throws the door open and looks out searchingly, waiting for Nathan to appear. But nothing.*)

(*He's really not coming back.* **MELODY** *starts to break, she hits herself in the head.*)

(*To herself.*) Stupid stupid stupid stupid stupid –

(**MELODY** *goes back to the worksheets she made for Nathan and tears them to shreds. She throws her backpack and worksheets at the wall in a rage.*)

(*Then a sound comes out of her very center – she screams, trying to make a scream that sounds like a scream of pain.**)

(*She screams.*)

(*She listens to it echo through the space.*)

(*Then screams again – this time trying to make a scream that sounds like a scream of pleasure.*)

(*She screams.*)

(*She listens to it echo too.*)

(*She tries pain again. Then pleasure again.*)

(*Then pain. She tries to hear the difference in her own voice.*)

(*Is there one?*)

(*Blackout.*)

---

* The number of screams in this scene may vary based on each production's staging needs and fight choreography. Please include at least three.

ACT TWO

Interlude V

(The Storage Room, eleven years later.)

(It looks the same as before, the discerning eye may notice rearranged items, chipping paint, and a layer of dust.)

(We wait for the door to open but it doesn't. Then, suddenly – the sound of a surge of electricity, and a bulb in the ceiling light explodes, and goes dark.)

Scene One

*(It's nighttime. The lock twists. **NATHAN** enters. Now, he's twenty-seven years old, and hiding something under his jacket.)*

*(**NATHAN** is wearing khakis, a slim tie, and a slightly wrinkled button-down shirt. He's got glasses on, coiffed hair, this is clearly his best effort to look put together.)*

(He takes in the room. Wow. He pockets his Swiss Army Knife – he used his old trick. He leaves the door ajar.)

(His coat is draped over his arm, he pulls it back to reveal an hors d'oeuvres plate, wrapped in plastic. He empties his pockets and takes out silverware, a handful of candy.)

(He lays everything out on the steel table and he sets a chair on either side. It's a pleasant picnic-style setup.)

(Then he darts to the dusty mirror to look at himself. He puts his blazer on. Then takes it back off. Then back on.)

(He turns to the wire rack and looks for his old box. He moves a box aside, and a sheet of dust falls into his face.)

*(Just then, the door swings open again – it's **MELODY**.)*

(She's wearing a chic dress and distinctive earrings, moving effortlessly in ambitious heels. She holds a sleek leather tote – like she's on the way home from work. She looks great and she knows it.)

(**NATHAN** *and* **MELODY** *lock eyes, the air is tense between them. Now, he is warm and gentle, she is cold and hardened. They recognize each other.*)

(*Then,* **NATHAN** *is overwhelmed by sneezes.*)

NATHAN. (*Sneezing.*) *** *** ***

MELODY. Uh, are you okay?

NATHAN. Yeah! Just / –

(*He sneezes.*)

*** I was looking for that old box, but then – *** Just, watch out, it's dusty in here –

(*While* **NATHAN** *finishes out his sneezing fit,* **MELODY** *takes in the space. It has a visceral effect on her that takes her by surprise. She's struck into silence for a moment.*)

(*Ventures.*) Hi.

MELODY. Hi.

(*Still taking in the room.*)

It's smaller than I remembered.

NATHAN. Or we're bigger.

(**MELODY** *shakes off the impact of the space and finally turns back to face him. He moves to meet her, their first good look at each other.*)

I wasn't sure if you'd come back here –

MELODY. I saw you slip out. And I was sick of all the small talk, the reunion coordinator lady had me cornered by the entrance, it was awful.

But I almost didn't recognize you. I mean, khakis.

NATHAN. You surprised I'm not a punk anymore?

MELODY. No – but I didn't expect a tie.

NATHAN. It's crooked.

MELODY. Just a little.

> (**MELODY** *scans* **NATHAN**, *taking him in the same way she took in the room.*)

Nathan Brancato.

NATHAN. Melody Martin.

MELODY. Nobody calls me Melody anymore.

In college I told everyone to call me "Mel," I never really liked Melody.

NATHAN. I didn't know that.

MELODY. *(Nonchalant.)* Oh yeah. Melody is just, so *hopeful* you know? It's a little girl's name.

So it's just easier to go with Mel, people take me more seriously –

NATHAN. I think your name is beautiful.

MELODY. *(Caught off-guard.)* Thanks.

> *(Changing the subject.)*

So was the box up there? When you checked?

> (**MELODY** *moves away from him and towards the wire rack.*)

NATHAN. I dunno, actually! Couldn't really see, with the dust and the – pain. I can try again –

> *(He moves back towards the rack and reaches up –)*

MELODY. That's – not a good idea. Just, hold on.

(**MELODY** *scans the space, then makes a plan: she takes a folding chair over to the wire rack, then steps up on the seat in her high heels to get a better look.*)

(*He looks up at her – his eyes trace the silhouette of her dress on the way. Their bodies are suddenly so close. He fumbles as he tries to occupy himself.*)

(**MELODY** *looks around, pokes at the boxes.*)

Hm. I don't see it. Sorry.

NATHAN. *(Surprised to be so sad.)* Oh. Too bad.

MELODY. Wow, you weren't kidding – it is dusty, I think they seriously *never* cleaned this room.

NATHAN. You're probably right. Don't touch anything, here –

(**NATHAN** *offers his hand to help her.*)

(**MELODY** *considers his hand, but doesn't take it. She steps down from the chair, gracefully, on her own.*)

(*Then* **MELODY** *moves toward the picnic setup he prepared.*)

MELODY. So what's all this?

(*She looks at the delicate setup again, the silverware laid out on custom-printed "10-year reunion" napkins.*)

NATHAN. Oh, I got it off the catering table, it's a special occasion.

MELODY. Well, actually – I have a little something too.

(**MELODY** *goes over to her professional tote and pulls out a bottle of champagne with pride.*)

NATHAN. Oh –!

MELODY. Pulled it from the stock bar, and I got glasses too.

(**MELODY** *takes two small plastic glasses out of her bag.*)

NATHAN. I'm impressed you fit a bottle in there.

MELODY. Oh, this is a *great* bag – it's my favorite, it holds much more than you'd think – it's a limited edition too! Great bag. Do you want a glass?

(**NATHAN** *shifts and seems uneasy.*)

NATHAN. Uh, maybe later. Honestly, I've had my eye on this candy –

(**NATHAN** *reaches out for the candy bar while* **MELODY** *puts down the bottle. She catches sight of* **NATHAN***'s hand.*)

MELODY. Oh my god – is that?

NATHAN. Oh, the scar?

(**NATHAN** *holds his hand up. There's a small white dot on his hand where the red cigarette burn mark used to be.*)

(**MELODY** *instinctively moves toward* **NATHAN***'s hand and holds it tenderly as she takes a closer look at the scar.*)

MELODY. I thought it would've faded.

NATHAN. It would've, if I'd taken care of it right.

MELODY. It's so round, it's like perfectly round.

NATHAN. Yeah, turns out a second-degree burn kills the blood vessels under it. Got bad circulation now, I gotta wear two gloves on it in the winter.

> *(Their bodies get close again, this time* **MELODY** *doesn't remove herself right away. She lingers near him.)*

MELODY. I'm sorry, I didn't mean to stare. It's really not bad, I'm sure nobody even notices it.

NATHAN. You notice everything.

> *(Heat. Then* **MELODY** *turns back to the champagne bottle.)*

MELODY. Anyway, where was I? Oh, champagne –

NATHAN. Uh hey, before I forget, did you see Jenny Wingate out there?

MELODY. In that disco-ball dress? How could I miss her.

NATHAN. Did you see the date she brought? With the tweed jacket, tall guy, bald spot?

He's her *second cousin*. Clint. I know that guy.

MELODY. *No way!*

NATHAN. Yup. Mother's side. Guess Jenny couldn't find a date.

> *(**MELODY** puts on a show of quieting her laughter.)*

MELODY. But. Y'know. We should go easy on her. We shouldn't joke.

NATHAN. Why not?

MELODY. *(Gravely.)* You mean you don't know? Jenny is sick.

She got this rare genetic thing – it's terminal.

MELODY. Didn't you see? She posts about it all the time, I thought everyone knew –

NATHAN. No, no – I'm not on any of that social media stuff – oh my god –!

MELODY. She has a surgery coming up, I'm surprised she even came out here tonight. So brave.

NATHAN. Brave, yes, totally – oh my god I'm so sorry, I didn't mean it like that –

(She watches him panic, then drops the act and laughs.)

MELODY. Relax. I'm fucking with you.

NATHAN. What?

MELODY. Jenny's fine. Outside of that freaky cousin thing. I'm sure she's still a terrible person, but she's not sick or whatever.

NATHAN. Oh. Wait – then, why did you say / that?

MELODY. So you're *really* not on social media?

NATHAN. *(Understanding.)* Oh. No, I'm not.

MELODY. Like – at all? None of it?

*(Beat. **NATHAN** leans back and smiles.)*

NATHAN. So you looked me up, huh?

(Beat. She's caught.)

MELODY. Tried to.

NATHAN. After high school I, uh – went off-grid for a while, deleted everything, and it stuck. I went back on once or twice, but every time I'd get a message from one of my brother's friends, or somebody that remembered me as a dealer. It just helped to unplug.

(Beat.)

But I looked you up too.

MELODY. You did?

NATHAN. I did. Impressive. I wasn't sure you'd even come tonight – since you're such a big shot.

MELODY. *(She knows exactly what he means.)* I don't know what you mean!

NATHAN. No, no – the internet had a lot to say about you! Wasn't it like: fancy undergrad, fancy fellowship, fancy MBA which got you your fancy corporate job – or did I scramble the steps? Aren't you like the CEO of some cutting-edge medical something?

MELODY. I'm a *junior* executive in product development at a biotechnology company, not a CEO

NATHAN. Okay fine, but that's like what – two steps away?

MELODY. ...three.

NATHAN. I'll give you five years, maybe four. And I saw that keynote speech you gave at that women in STEM thing, it was great! I'm sure it's only a matter of time before you run for Congress or / something –

MELODY. Okay, / okay –

NATHAN. And then the inevitable book deal, talk show, the Nobel Peace Prize, / Medal of Honor –

MELODY. Oh, so now I'm gonna solve world peace? –

NATHAN. You could! You're doing big things, you got everything you wanted.

MELODY. Well –

NATHAN. What?

MELODY. I dunno. Sometimes it doesn't feel like I imagined it would.

(**MELODY** *is lost in thought for a moment,*
NATHAN *watches her searchingly. Then,*
she remembers herself and puts on a smile,
snapping back into her charming mode.)

MELODY. God, now I'm *really* ready for that drink. And
anyway – I think it's your turn! You looked me up but
I couldn't look you up, so you have to fill me in. Here –

(**MELODY** *pours two glasses of champagne*
and hands one to **NATHAN**. *He reaches out*
toward the cup – then stops himself short,
clamming up.)

You okay? What, are you driving?

NATHAN. I actually, um. I don't drink anymore.

MELODY. Oh.

NATHAN. Sorta got my shit together about three years ago.

(*Long beat.* **MELODY** *looks at the glasses in*
her hands.)

MELODY. Is it cool if like – *I* drink it.

NATHAN. Oh, absolutely! I work at a restaurant with a bar
– please, go ahead.

MELODY. *Great.* Restaurant! Start there.

(**MELODY** *pours the champagne from his*
glass into hers. She takes a seat in one of the
chairs and quizzes him.)

NATHAN. Sure uh – I work in the kitchen at Seasonado
down on Main Street now. It's small, but upscale – we
get good reviews, at least. It's like "New American"
fusion stuff.

MELODY. You're a chef?

NATHAN. Oh, I'm a *cook* – chefs go to culinary school. But I'm starting soon! Hopefully in a few months. I'm gonna take the classes part-time, I can do it in a year or two. Here, allow me.

> (**NATHAN** *dramatically peels the plastic off the hors d'oeuvres tray. He makes them a plate.*)

I was waiting tables and I made friends with some guys in the kitchen, got interested. It's an accepting industry – plenty of people with a past, you know? I mean, it takes a certain personality to want to spend twelve hours on your feet in a hot room full of people shouting. I'm basically a line cook, I make soup all day, but at least I get to work with my hands. Here you go –

> (**NATHAN** *hands her the plate,* **MELODY** *takes it.*)

MELODY. I feel like we should toast, but you don't have anything –

NATHAN. Oh, I brought uh –

> (**NATHAN** *pulls out a can of sparkling water. He holds it up to toast.*)

MELODY. To...? The past? Or – the present! Or like...our good health or whatever.

NATHAN. Maybe you should stick to keynote speeches, you're not great at toasting.

MELODY. You make it then!

NATHAN. To...the dust in this room. To old times, and new beginnings. To seeing you again.

> (*Heat.*)

> (*Clink – they toast.*)

(**MELODY** *sips her drink and starts to pick at
her plate of food. But* **NATHAN** *is preoccupied.
He puts down his glass and leans in toward*
MELODY.)

NATHAN. Melody, I actually, uh – I actually, wanted to see
you here tonight for a reason.

MELODY. You did?

NATHAN. Yeah. I wanted to tell you, um. I've been thinking
a lot, and like –

(**NATHAN** *clears his throat.*)

Whewh, the dust is uh, intense in here.

MELODY. It's okay, like – take your time.

(**NATHAN** *takes a nervous sip and begins
again.*)

NATHAN. I've been thinking a lot about you, and about
high school, and – I wanted to tell you.

(**NATHAN** *takes a deep breath.*)

That I'm sorry. I'm so so sorry, for, just – all of it.

(**MELODY** *shifts.*)

I'm sorry for who I was back then. Like, I was such
an asshole about those worksheets – god, you're like
the whole reason I even graduated and I never even
thanked you for that. Never even did the simple thing
of thanking you. And I couldn't piece it together until I
finally sobered up and got my act together –

MELODY. Wait, wait, wait – is this? Are you doing a
12-Step thing –?

NATHAN. Something like it. You know 'em?

MELODY. Old boyfriend.

So – is this a recovery apology? This is *amends*?

NATHAN. Well – yes and no. I do want to make amends, but that's not the only reason I'm apologizing, if that makes sense.

(**MELODY** *tenses in her chair.*)

MELODY. Well then, I'm glad you got that off your chest, and checked me off your little list –

NATHAN. Checked you off? No –!

MELODY. – and now that you have, I think we should just / drop it.

NATHAN. Melody I'm not just trying to check you off a list, really!

It was important to me to apologize to you. I've changed, I want to make things right –

(*Suddenly,* **MELODY** *stands and launches away from the table. She starts hunting around the space, poking at the stacks of storage boxes that litter the room.*)

(*She tries to put on her cocktail party voice – upbeat and perfectly pleasant.*)

MELODY. You know what – I'm willing to bet you that box is still in here!

NATHAN. Melody –?

MELODY. Maybe not up there, but I'm sure it's still here somewhere – it's gotta be.

Maybe things got changed around, somebody tried to reorganize and just threw it into a corner somewhere. I see cardboard! Want to look for it?

NATHAN. Did you hear what I just said?

MELODY. Yes. I assumed you were finished with that – were you finished?

NATHAN. I mean, not quite –

MELODY. Look, you said what you wanted to say, and I hope you feel better now.

Or whatever it is you wanted to feel –

NATHAN. No, this is for you, this is about you! I'm sorry, I think I didn't phrase myself right –

> (**MELODY**'s *façade breaks – she rounds on him.*)

MELODY. No, I don't think you did phrase it right, honestly. Amends for the academic dishonesty, for your B– in Chem? The worksheets? Is that what you're really sorry for?

> (*Beat.* **NATHAN** *sighs and puts his head in his hands.*)

NATHAN. I didn't mean it like that.

MELODY. So? …

NATHAN. God, you can still see right through me.

There were so many fuckups – I'm not quite sure where to start.

MELODY. Well start again.

> (**NATHAN** *considers it and takes a deep breath.*)

NATHAN. I'm screwing this up too, huh?

Back then I just – destroyed things. I destroyed the good things in my life, because I hated the world, hated myself –

> (**MELODY** *stops him again.*)

MELODY. You keep talking about yourself, if you're trying to apologize to me, apologize to *me* –

NATHAN. That's what I meant! Like, I took that out on you, all my bullshit! I know that I became a better person at your expense, and that was so unfair to you!

For a while there you were the only person in the world who even cared if I lived or died.

MELODY. No I wasn't.

NATHAN. Yeah you were! I put a cigarette through my hand and nobody looked twice except for you.

MELODY. That's really fucked up Nathan.

NATHAN. Yeah, it is. But it's true.

MELODY. Okay. Like is that, is that really all you want to say to me?

NATHAN. I mean, that's why I wanted to apologize, to thank you!

MELODY. But like – is that all?

NATHAN. I mean, I can keep going! I just, uh. I guess I don't know what you want me to say.

(**MELODY** *drops the act.*)

MELODY. Nathan, the last time we were in this room together you like –

You asked me how I would know what it was like for someone to want me.

You stood right there, and you laughed in my face, you threw a handful of cash at me, you made me feel like shit. You don't want to apologize for that?

(*Long beat.* **NATHAN** *sinks into his chair.*)

NATHAN. I don't remember that.

MELODY. Are you serious? You don't remember that day?

NATHAN. I know we had a fight, I know that you were mad at me but the rest is like – blurry, it was so long ago. I just. I didn't remember that.

MELODY. Well I do, I remember.

NATHAN. Fuck, that's so scary –

MELODY. Like every shitty thought I ever had about myself and you confirmed it –

NATHAN. I didn't know what I was saying, I was just caught up –

MELODY. And it especially fucking hurt because I was the only Black girl at this school and I was so alone here –

NATHAN. – Right, of course –

MELODY. – And everyone thought I was weird, and I always knew that in the back of my head but nobody ever said it to my face, and then you did! I thought you were my friend.

NATHAN. You're right, I should've known better, I was awful to you – I didn't even think about what it was like for you. I just – I'm so sorry. Fuck, Melody, I'm *so* sorry!

MELODY. It's been ringing in my head for ten years and it was nothing for you.

NATHAN. Not nothing! I never forgot you! I never forgot this room!

> (**MELODY** *is struggling to keep her composure.*)

MELODY. You know what?

This was a bad idea, I don't know what I was thinking –

> (**MELODY** *moves to gather her things and leave the room.*)

NATHAN. Wait, Melody don't go – we can talk it through!

MELODY. No, this isn't going anywhere, this is just one of *those* times, where I cared and cared about people who never give a damn about me, well I don't do that anymore!

(**NATHAN** *corrects her.*)

NATHAN. Melody, I was crazy about you in high school.

(*Beat.* **MELODY** *goes still.*)

MELODY. What?

NATHAN. I had feelings for you in high school, of course I did.

MELODY. Oh.

NATHAN. That's what I meant! Fuck, I knew I wasn't explaining it right.

That fight? That's what I meant about destroying the good things. You were the good.

(**MELODY** *sounds suddenly gentle, an echo of high school.*)

MELODY. I was?

NATHAN. Of course. Look, I can't pretend I didn't see that you were different – not just different in this school of rich white assholes, but different because you were like, real.

MELODY. Why didn't you say anything to me?

NATHAN. I don't know. That seemed impossible, like it would've been easier to fly to the moon.

MELODY. But why? If you felt it.

NATHAN. I didn't want to feel anything back then, I just wanted to be like, numb.

NATHAN. Part of it was just paranoia – keeping everyone at a distance, pushing them away before they could realize what a piece of shit I was and push *me* away. Honestly, I thought I was doing you a favor –

MELODY. Yeah great fucking favor.

NATHAN. You're right. I just, didn't know how to like say what I felt – I still don't, honestly. I'm learning. But of course I liked you then.

(Realizing.) Wait, I can show you, hold on! Do you remember this?

> *(**NATHAN** takes a piece of paper out of his wallet and shows it to her. It's the note with her lipstick kiss from Act One. **MELODY** stops in her tracks.)*

MELODY. Is that –?

NATHAN. I kept it. You slipped it into my bag, you remember? I don't even know how you pulled that off – how you got so close to me without me realizing.

MELODY. I thought you never got it, or you threw it away or something.

I thought I imagined this whole thing.

NATHAN. No – I mean, I kept coming back didn't I? That was *huge* for me!

I didn't do anything routine like that – there were a couple of days I cut every class but showed up for lunch just to see you.

> *(**MELODY** laughs, she softens.)*

But I mean, you were like, this was my whole –

I'm uh – I'm rambling, I'm sorry. I haven't talked like this in years, not since you.

But, Melody, of course I cared about you in high school. I think the reason I held on to this note for so long is because it's the closest I ever got to kissing you.

> *(Heat.)*

> *(**MELODY** takes a small step toward him, consciously narrowing the space between them. Then another.)*

> *(**NATHAN** moves in too – they're close enough to whisper.)*

So I guess –

I guess *that's* what I'm really sorry about. I wish I'd kissed you then.

I wish I'd told you how much I wanted you.

MELODY. So tell me now –

NATHAN. I want you.

> *(**MELODY** kisses **NATHAN**.)*

> *(**NATHAN** is shocked, **MELODY** is swept away.)*

> *(At first it's like the clumsy high school kiss that never was. They're teenagers again, awkward and intrepid.)*

> *(Then, it becomes all-consuming – he takes her waist, she wraps her arms around his neck. Closeness, heat.)*

> *(In wordless agreement, they begin to shuffle towards the metal table in the center of the room. She starts to loosen his tie, pulling it off of his body.)*

> *(They whisper to each other in gasps between kisses, trying to catch their breath.)*

NATHAN. – I – I can't believe I'm seeing you here again –

MELODY. – I know, come here –

> *(**MELODY** moves back toward the steel table and pulls him along with her – but **NATHAN** wants to talk, he's overcome with conviction.)*

NATHAN. Wait, Melody I want to be with you.

MELODY. Then get over here –

> *(She beckons him to join her on the table.)*

> *(He takes her by the waist and pulls back from her lips.)*

NATHAN. No, no, I mean for real –

Like, outside this room, like – what if we do this thing for real?

> *(Beat.)*

MELODY. What?

NATHAN. I know I'm rushing things, getting ahead of myself, classic –

MELODY. What are you talking about?

NATHAN. I'm talking about us! I'm talking / about *this* –

MELODY. Can we just – talk later –?

NATHAN. This is how I fucked up last time, not *saying* – not *saying* what I meant, I won't make that mistake again.

> *(**MELODY** pulls back from him.)*

MELODY. Nathan –

NATHAN. Wait, just listen – I'm not saying I have a right to be in your life, but fuck I *want* to!

MELODY. What?

NATHAN. Melody I want to know you again, I want to hear your voice.

I know this is a lot, I just think we owe it to ourselves to talk about it, at least –

(**MELODY** *makes space between them – she moves away from the table and begins to pace.*)

MELODY. There isn't anything to talk about!

NATHAN. Why not?

MELODY. Because – you don't mean it. You're not serious.

NATHAN. Yes I am – I do!

MELODY. You couldn't possibly be! Nathan it's been over ten years – like, have you lost your mind?

NATHAN. Look, I feel stupid even asking, looking at your life and mine. I never would've thought, if you hadn't kissed me –

MELODY. Nathan –

NATHAN. Just – picture it, just for even a second, will you?

I know you're in the city now – but I don't mind the drive! I can do it in an hour, easy breezy. I'll get into audiobooks, finally!

(**MELODY** *laughs, against her better judgement.*)

And we could – catch up. Except we won't just have an hour until the school bell calls us back to class, we can talk until the sun comes up, and fill in all the gaps.

We could get a dog!

MELODY. A dog?!

NATHAN. Yeah! You know, down the line or whatever. I always wanted a big goofy retriever, but I'm open! We can get like a little midsize shorthair poodle if you want – or a cat even, if you're a cat person!

MELODY. I like big goofy dogs.

NATHAN. See, it could work! Oh, and I can cook for you, show off my signature soup!

I got a butternut squash, french onion, matzo ball – what do you like?

> (**MELODY** *is overwhelmed and makes space between them.* **NATHAN**'s *appeal takes on a manic quality.*)

MELODY. I dunno, this is crazy – like, we have whole different lives now, both of us.

NATHAN. We'll figure it out! We can make it work!

MELODY. Just, can we slow down? Shouldn't we start with like, a date?

NATHAN. Why date when we already know each other like this!

MELODY. Like what?! I know you did some research or whatever but like, it's been over ten years – you don't know the first thing about me!

NATHAN. Yes I do!

MELODY. Oh yeah? What's my mother's name?

> (*Beat.* **NATHAN** *doesn't know.*)

That's what I'm talking about! You don't know my friends, or my allergies, or my favorite books – like, you have no idea who I am now.

NATHAN. But I know who you were, in this room! And you haven't changed –

MELODY. A lot has changed, actually.

NATHAN. Then I want to learn!

MELODY. And I don't know you either.

NATHAN. But you do, you know me better than anyone.

MELODY. We're not in high school anymore Nathan!

NATHAN. Alright alright – of course we can go on dates, we can go anywhere!

I just mean, like. I feel so good around you! We're good together! Don't you feel that?

(**MELODY** *begins to feel uneasy.*)

MELODY. I don't know.

NATHAN. I feel amazing, I haven't felt alive like this for years.

MELODY. This doesn't make sense –

NATHAN. Look – there are plenty of reasons to have doubts – I know I have a shitty past, I know I hurt you. Honestly, I never thought that anyone could see me – see beyond the damage, and want me anyway.

MELODY. Don't say that.

NATHAN. Say what?

MELODY. You're not damaged.

NATHAN. Believe me, I am.

MELODY. Everyone has a past.

NATHAN. Not a past like mine.

MELODY. But that's not –

(*She catches herself.*)

Wait.

> (**MELODY**'s *face twists up. She pulls away from him.*)

NATHAN. What's wrong?

MELODY. Why am I comforting you?

NATHAN. Because you're an angel!

MELODY. I'm not a fucking angel Nathan!

NATHAN. You have a good heart! You're generous, I love talking to you, you make me a better man.

MELODY. And that's why you want to be with me?

NATHAN. Yes, exactly!

MELODY. Nathan, none of that is about me, it's about you.

NATHAN. No it's not.

MELODY. You like me because I make you feel good, that's not about me.

NATHAN. No, but like – you're taking it out of context, I'm trying to tell you how much I appreciate you! Your kindness was beyond what I deserved, and it changed me!

MELODY. You keep talking about high school like I was some kind of saint, but I wasn't – I was just a girl. I was a lonely teenage girl, and you let me down, and that's worse.

NATHAN. It wasn't all bad, was it?

> (**MELODY** *breaks.*)

MELODY. *(Snapping at him.)* Why couldn't we just fuck on that table and go our separate ways!

NATHAN. This was more than that, you said it yourself –!

MELODY. I just wanted to do a victory lap and put it all behind me, because sad little Melody is all grown up now, and she grew up a winner. And you couldn't just let me have that!

NATHAN. Then why are you still here with me?

Why did you bring me a bottle of champagne?

Why did you kiss me?

MELODY. I don't know!

> *(She looks down at herself and finds that she's shaking, buzzing with energy. She starts to pace across the room.)*

NATHAN. Admit it – you came here tonight for the same reason you came ten years ago. You're missing something. Something that doesn't exist out there. We found it before, together.

MELODY. What we *found* in here was not good for me!

You hiding from me in the hallways but getting all close to me in this room like I was some kind of back-shed secret? And you did it again!

You didn't wave to me out there in the fucking auditorium – no! You had to lead me back here like prey from the pack, away from Jenny and her stupid dress and all those eyes. And I followed you. I followed you. Again.

You think *you* had a self-destructive pattern?!

I had a self-destructive pattern Nathan, and it was *you*!

> *(**MELODY** is still reeling, **NATHAN** charges in.)*

NATHAN. You're not happy Melody –

MELODY. You don't know what you're talking about –

NATHAN. If you were you wouldn't be in here with me!

I recognize the signs because I'm not happy either.

MELODY. That's not my problem!

NATHAN. I know that I hurt you, but I can make up for that now. I see how cold you've become now, how many walls you've put up –

MELODY. Fuck you Nathan –

NATHAN. And I know I'm responsible for that, I trained you / to close off.

MELODY. / You think you *trained* me? –

NATHAN. But I've changed, I'm a new man now –

MELODY. / Will you just stop, just shut the fuck up! –

NATHAN. And now I know I can make this right –

> (**MELODY** *charges at* **NATHAN** *and screams in his face –*)
>
> (*It sounds so human – halfway between the pain scream and the pleasure scream, like an echo, or an exorcism. A scream of power.*)
>
> (*The scream lands in* **NATHAN**, *lands in* **MELODY**, *and lands in the room.* **NATHAN** *falls silent, stunned. A quiet, still moment.*)
>
> (*She returns to the ten-year-old note with her lipstick kiss.*)

MELODY. (*She realizes.*) Oh. That's it –

I thought my heart was pounding because of you, but really it's this whole building.

Every day I came to this school, during that hour on the bus I would get this tight feeling in my chest. I felt it on the drive up from the city today too.

I felt so small here. I thought if I could just twist myself into the right shape then people would accept me – and it would be worth it no matter how much it hurt.

And then there was you, and this one room where I could catch my breath. You were never a good friend to me, but that one shred of kindness was all I had.

At sixteen this was everything I ever wanted but now? It's not enough.

> (**MELODY** *gives back the note with her lipstick kiss.*)

> (**MELODY** *is hit with a sense of clarity, like the spell is broken. She packs up her things to leave.*)

> (**MELODY** *collects her bag and coat,* **NATHAN** *is stunned.*)

> (*She's halfway out the door when she stops and turns back, the bottle of champagne has caught her eye.*)

This is mine –

> (*She grabs it and moves for the door decisively, her heels clicking with each step.*)

> (*Click, click, click, click –*)

NATHAN. Melody –

> (**MELODY** *turns around and looks at him one last time.*)

> (*Then* **MELODY** *leaves the Storage Room without hesitation. The heavy metal door closes with a thud behind her.*)

> (**NATHAN** *is alone.*)

Interlude VI

(The final beats overlap. Moments later:)

(**NATHAN** –)

(Takes in the empty room, and the kiss note in his hand.)

(**MELODY** –)

(Moves through the parking lot, almost out of breath from marching herself out of the reunion.)

(On impulse, she takes out a cigarette and sparks her lighter. She puts the cigarette between her lips and holds up the flame – then she stops herself.)

(**MELODY** *lets go of the flame, puts the cigarette back in the pack, and tosses it all into her bag.)*

(**NATHAN** –)

(Traces the napkin kiss with his finger one last time. Then he puts it gently back down on the table.)

(**MELODY** –)

(Takes off her heels and throws them in the back seat of her car, finally ready to start the trip back home. She leaves the school building behind.)

(NATHAN –)

(Picks up his coat and exits, leaving the closet and his mementos behind.)

(MELODY –)

(Rolls down her window and feels the wind in her hair.)

(She takes a deep breath.)

(Blackout.)

End of Play

Printed in the USA
CPSIA information can be obtained
at www.ICGtesting.com
JSHW011433201124
73976JS00010B/56

9 780573 710926